ZOO BOY and the Jewel Thieves

A story with songs...

SOPHIE THOMPSON

is an Olivier Award-winning actress. Her films include *Harry Potter and the Deathly Hallows*, *Emma*, *Persuasion* and *Four Weddings and a Funeral*. On stage Sophie has appeared in many plays and musicals at the National Theatre, with the RSC and in the West End. Her television roles have included *The Detectorists*, *Jericho* and *EastEnders*. Sophie won *Celebrity MasterChef* in 2014 and wrote the cookbook *My Family Kitchen: Favourite recipes from four generations*. She has two teenage sons and lives in North London. *Zoo Boy and the Jewel Thieves* is the second story in the Zoo Boy series.

ZOO BOY
and the
Jewel Thieves

A story with songs ...

SOPHIE THOMPSON

Illustrated by **Rebecca Ashdown**

ff

FABER & FABER

First published in 2017
by Faber & Faber Limited
Bloomsbury House, 74–77 Great Russell Street
London WC1B 3DA

Typeset by Faber & Faber Limited
Printed and bound in the UK by CPI Group UK (Ltd)
Croydon CRO 4YY

A CIP record for this book is available
from the British Library

ISBN 978–0–571–32520–7

For Ernie, Walter, Gaia,

Tindy and Elbie

Prologue

Hello, dear reader.

Are you sitting, lying down, standing on your head, eating a jam sandwich comfortably?

Then I'll begin . . .

I want to introduce you to a boy called Vince. Some of you might have met him before, so you must forgive me if I am repeating myself – but for those of you who don't know him, not very long ago and far away, on his eighth birthday, Vince discovered he could talk to animals.

I know!

What a turn-up!

And this is a boy who previously didn't even like animals!

Life can be very cheeky, can't it?

Anyway. Vince lives at number 21 Alberkirky Street, and his house

backs on to the zoo where his dad is the zoo keeper. In fact there is a gate at the bottom of their garden that lets them into the zoo – once they have sung the secret Zoo Keepers' Song, obviously.

Vince's dad has cheered up no end since Vince's talking-to-animals revelation. He had been a bit blue, you see, as Vince's mum recently ran off with the circus, and (more to the point) a lion-taming man called Reg, who is very muscly and has no sense of humour (tragic).

Vince's gran also lives at number 21. Gran used to be an entertainer and travel around the country, dancing and singing in pubs and clubs with a troupe called The Moonbeams. She is a wonderful woman – I think you would get on. Gran gets on with everybody, except, coincidentally, with someone in this story who you shall hear more about in a moment.

I'm pretty sure that's all you need to know for now about the residents of number 21 Alberkirky Street, dear reader – so now I can start to tell you about Vince's new adventure . . .

One

Six a.m. Greenwich Mean Time.
(Why 'Mean'? Let's call it 'Generous
Time'.)

A blue light wiped across Vince's
closed eyes and BLAP! he was
awake!

What was that? Vince wondered,
padding to the window.

It was a police car, parked at number 19, right next door, where Mrs Footlecrannoch lived.

Mrs Footlecrannoch was a rather unapproachable smarty-pants lady, who apparently had inherited a lot of money from a relative who sold heaters (that wouldn't melt igloos) to Eskimos. She wore a different hat daily, and she also had a plethora of JEWELS, but she never wore them because

they were far too precious. Which just seemed plain silly to Gran. I mean, what is the point of THAT? Gran's jewels are only pretend, but she wears them all the time. She says (very wisely, I think) that she doesn't need the excuse of a special occasion because every day is a special occasion.

Just as Vince was wondering what had happened, Gerry the local copper emerged from Mrs Footlecrannoch's elaborate front door.

'Don't you worry, Mrs F., we'll get your precious jewels returned in no time – I feel sure of it.'

'I will pay a substantial reward: all the Swiss roll they can eat!' Mrs Footlecrannoch exclaimed, spluttering like a tap with a wonky washer.

Well, there was an offer. Vince had always quite fancied being a super sleuth, and he had always been particularly partial to a bit of Swiss roll.

So he got his diary (called Derek) off the shelf, and started a new entry.

Dear Derek,

There has been a robbery – would you believe it? – right next door to our house!

I have decided I must crack the case, and I will be employing some of my ~~freinds~~ friends at the zoo to help me (I hope). You can be my Investigation Notebook. All super sl~~o~~euths must take notes while looking very serious and scratching their heads. I am going to do all of these things. Let's go!

Vince got dressed and put Derek into his pocket, along with a pencil and a small magnifying glass that had come in his stamp collection kit (all super sleuths magnified things, it was a well-known fact). Then, feeling very important and curiously clever, he strode off with an expression of fantastic determination on his face.

Once he got to the bottom of the garden, he let himself into the zoo with the secret Zoo Keepers' Song.

Horace the badger greeted him at the other side of the gate. (In case you are wondering, Horace is wild, but chooses to live at the zoo. This is because secretly he's rather fond of all the animals.)

'I smelt you approaching,' Horace proffered.

'Charming!' said Vince.

'Don't worry, you're extremely

fragrant. I'm just a champ at smelling,' retorted Horace rather haughtily, adding, 'You look very pinky and perky for this time in the morning. What's occurring?'

'There's been a jewel robbery next door at Mrs Footlecrannoch's.'

'You're not serious?' said Horace.

'Yes! The police were there just now, but I want to solve the crime because Mrs Footlecrannoch is offering Swiss roll as a reward.'

'I meant you're not serious

about that ridiculous name! Mrs Footlecrannoch? Were her parents comedians?'

Vince tried to remain focused. 'Let's confer with the group, Horace. See who would be a worthy side salad – I mean sidekick.'

Horace was unimpressed.

'Jewel thieves, super sleuths . . . hold your horses! Just because you can talk to animals now, it doesn't mean you're suddenly going to become Colin the Cream Cracker – I mean, Crime Cracker. But by the way, I do happen to have a rather fetching cape . . .' he added meaningfully.

'I think it's only fair that I open this job opportunity up to the group,' Vince replied.

'Spoilsport,' chuntered Horace. 'Why does everything have to be "fair"?'

Two

Vince and Horace found Asquith the penguin over by the pool, painting his nails cerise pink.

'Now there's a sight I didn't expect to see today!' Vince exclaimed.

'Always happy to surprise!' said Asquith proudly. 'Your metaphorical tail looks very fluffy, have you something thrilling to impart, dear boy?'

'Well!' said Vince, trying to sound as dramatic as possible. 'There's been a local robbery and I want to solve the crime, but I need a seaside – I mean sidekick. It's traditional for super sleuths to have one.'

'Ooooh, I do love a mystery,' said Asquith. 'In fact, do you think it's too early on in the story for a song? I happen to know a good 'un about crime!'

'No time like the present!' said Vince. 'I think a song is a MUST.'

'I beg to differ,' Horace muttered darkly.

Asquith cleared his throat and folded a flipper across his puffed-out shiny chest.

I once knew a 'tea leaf' (thief)

Who couldn't control his needs.

He stole from every quarter,

Even nicked sweets from his daughter!

He took his auntie Joan's kazoo

And all the jokes from Uncle Tone,

He took his grannie Annie's loo

Plus all the ice cream off her cone.

He took the moos from several cows,

He took the smile from cousin Trish,

He took a lion from his roar

And lots of tails from lots of fish.

20

He took the pointy bits from stars

And from the sun he took some rays,

He took an alien from Mars

And from last week he took two days.

Then what occurred you won't believe,

He started taking from himself!

Took his fingers and his thumbs,

All the teeth from out his gums.

And sad but true that was his end.

He robbed his heart, his bones, his skin,

He took it ALL until the day . . .

That there was NOTHING left of him.

'Well, that's a jolly ditty, I must say,' grumbled Horace.

'Very illuminating,' said Vince. 'But are you sure you're the best man – I mean penguin – for the job?'

'No! I'd be dreadful!' said Asquith, rather surprisingly.

'That was rather surprising,' said Horace.

'I'm just not efficient enough when it comes to dry land. I think it's always best to know one's limitations, and I would hold you back, dear boy.'

'Well, I admire your honesty, Asquith,' said Vince.

'I don't,' rumbled Horace. 'It certainly won't get you very far in the workplace,' he added knowingly. 'NEXT!' he barked.

Word had got round . . .

There was a GIANT queue for the job interview.

Three

Vince fished Derek the diary from  his pocket and took notes as each animal proffered up his or her skills. Oh, Vince did love a list . . .

Asquith (penguin)
very good song, but
unreliable on dry land
by own ~~admishun~~ admission.
Job: would make fine
commander of base camp
team here at zoo. Has a dashing
line in waistcoats, plus a clipboard
apparently. Displays
natural authority.

Terry (orangutan)
good effort, had

gone to a lot of trouble with his hair, but just recited a dodgy poem about his bogies. Job: has offered to plan celebratory party for when we return (triumphant obvs.).
Good idea — he's proper nifty on the

ZOOM

bongos.

Hamish (eagle) and Janet (owl) did lots of swooping

and shrieking and then stuffed their faces with insects.

Job: they say they're extremely good at stealth. Looked it up in pocket dictionary. It means cautious
~~cowshus~~ and surreptishus action tious
or movement. Perfect! They can be the look outs, as wings clearly handy too.

Carol (pig)
performed truly

curious tap dance around Asquith's pond whilst singing ancient Cornish sea shanty. Job: says she's very wise. Think she should come with. Would do her confidence no end of good.

Juan (llama) gave bizarre recital in a rather flamboyant poncho. It went like this:

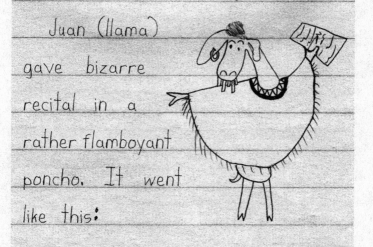

On Monday I take my love
on a boat,
But alas and alack
sheee threw up
All over her shooooes!
Eet was terrible news,
Sheeee had eeeeaten too much
ketchup.

On Tuesday I take my love
on a train,
Alas and alack
sheeee threw up again!

30

Too much ice creeeeam and sauce,
So weeee went home of course.

On Wednesday weeee get
on a plane,
Eeeet was all looking good,
Till came theee plane food,
And the sauce on theeeee
chicken too thick . . .
(You've spotted theee rhyme . . .)
In next to no time,
My poncho was covered
eeen sick!

I know! Weird! That's something I won't forget in a hurry, Derek. Job: Terry thinks Juan should stay and be part of the entertainment later. Can't help but agree. He's very dramatic! (He's had experience as a pantomime llama.)

Dave (goat) just told lots of bad jokes. Job: entertainment, deffo.

Fenella (flamingo) sang us all a song about how wonderful she is . . . Ha ha. But she has a walkie-talkie set that works! She's in!

Hello? hello!

33

Dear reader, I might have to find a moment to write Fenella's song down for you. She is such a frightful big-head, it did make me laugh. Maybe if we have got time at the end of this story and the Powers That Be allow . . .

Four

Just as the job interviews drew to a close, Gran appeared with a large box of liquorice allsorts.

She was casually attired in a lemon-yellow sheath dress and a feather fascinator, and she looked like she had some very pressing news to impart, as her lips were all juddery

and her brow extra wrinkled.

'Greetings, my awesome animal cracker and his glorious pals. I knew

I would find you here!' she exclaimed, sounding rather emotional. 'Vincey, my princey – guess what! That silly old moo Mrs Footlecrannoch has been robbed! Gerry the local PC Plod has just been round asking questions. I nearly fainted – he was eyeing up all my jewels, the cheeky blighter. I assured him they were fake and that I was innocent, but I don't think he believed me – I feel tainted by his suspicious glare! It's playing havoc with my sugar levels so I've had to hit the allsorts!'

Vince jumped in. 'Gran! I know about the robbery! I've been holding job interviews for my sidecar – I mean sidekick. I am to be a super sleuth and we are going to solve the crime! We will clear your name, find Mrs Footlecrannoch's jewels and apparently get all the Swiss roll we can eat to boot!'

Gran's expression lightened and the sparkle came back into her eyes.

'Oh, my diamond geezer, I knew

you would lift my day, just like a human support stocking!' Gran looked like she might cry, and there ensued a frightful hullabaloo as all the animals piped up to try and make her feel better – but of course she didn't understand a word of it.

'What are they all saying, Vincey, jewel of my heart?'

'They are now even more determined to crack this case, Gran! They are also being very rude about Mrs Footlecrannoch on your behalf.'

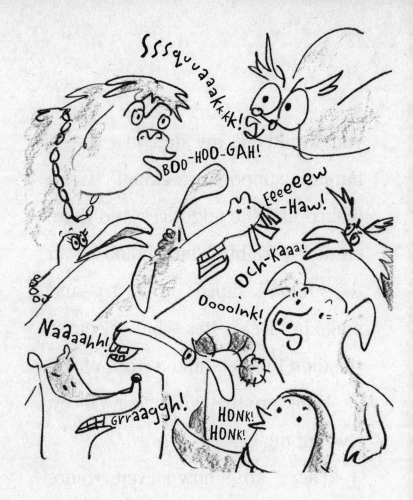

(Gran tried not to look too pleased about this.) 'I've assembled a corking team, Gran, worry thee not.'

'Oh, I do love a good sleuth! Especially a YOU-shaped one! What's the plan?'

'Ah!' declared Vince. 'We haven't quite got that far . . .'

Five

Dingley dongley dannger lannger bongey bungey raddley ruddley beeeeeep! went Mrs Footlecrannocch's ridiculously flamboyant bell.

Vince and Horace stood side by side on the front step, both wearing shiny capes – Vince's was pillarbox red and Horace's bluebottle black.

Behind them were Fenella and Carol, dressed in an ill-fitting variety of Gran's clothes. They looked like a couple of very small magicians with their glamorous assistants.

Mrs Footlecrannoch came to the door looking rather tearful and a lot less game than she did on a normal Thursday. She had very bad eyesight and wore specs so thick her eyes looked like two fat floppy fish. She was sporting a wide-brimmed straw hat trimmed with cherries.

'Hello, Vincent Norman Ligglethwaite . . . and friends,' she said, peering hard at them with her swimmy eyes.

Mrs Footlecrannoch always used all your names when she addressed you. Most odd. And an awful time-waster for Leviticus Corkindale Percival Calamine Periwig Candlewick Throooob, who ran the local shop, did deliveries and was often in a ridiculous hurry.

Vince cut to the chase. 'Mrs Footlecrannoch, me and my sidecar – I mean sideboard – I mean SIDEKICK . . .'

'Get a grip!' rumbled Horace

darkly, adjusting his cape.

Vince continued undeterred: '. . . and our attractive assistants would like to offer our crime-solving services at a cut-price rate, seeing as it is the first Thursday of the month.'

'How utterly divine!' said Mrs Footlecrannoch. 'Do come up and survey the scene of the dastardly deed.'

She led them upstairs to her

bedroom, which was a riot of drapes and tassels.

'Take a look over here, if you will. I'll put the kettle on, I am aware you workers like a brew.' And with that Mrs F. left our unexpected four to their sleuthing.

Vince and Horace began to take a very good gander about, while Fenella and Carol wandered around Mrs Footlecrannoch's bedroom in absolute awe.

'Oh, how often I have dreamt

of having a ridiculous amount of drapery!' Fenella exclaimed.

'Oh, how I have wished, every Wednesday at least, for chocolates in my sty!' grunted Carol, clocking an enormous box of chocs by Mrs Footlecrannoch's bed and trying to maintain strict control.

'Concentrate, girls!' blustered Horace. 'Observe!'

On the floor by an open window was some evidence. Here it shall be listed as Vince wrote it in Derek:

A red leather jewel box – overturned and empty!

Some strands of grey hair

A biscuit crumb or three

A middle-sized white feather

A large black feather

A shiny, slightly sticky re̶s̶i̶d̶e̶w̶ residue (unpleasant)

Quite a lot of fluff

(I'm no detective, dear reader, but my guess is Mrs Footlecrannoch was not on very good terms with her Hoover)

A yellow elastic band

A Milky Way wrapper

A small lump of blue plasticine

Suddenly the walkie-talkie that Fenella had secreted in her feathers puckled into action.

'One two! One two! Come in please, super sleuths and attractive assistants – over, dudes!' It was

Terry the orangutan. 'Have you solved the crime yet? Over. If not, why not, man? Over.'

'Don't be absurd!' Horace spluttered into the walkie-talkie, having snatched it from Fenella, who was too busy being mesmerised by her own reflection in Mrs Footlecrannoch's full-length mirror. 'We've only just got here! This is a complicated business – there's a lot of profundity to ponder and clues to clarify, you oaf!'

'There's no need for that,' piped up Vince. 'We are a team, we all pull our weight.'

'I wouldn't want to be pulling Terry's weight, that's for sure,' Horace grouched.

'Tea time!' warbled Mrs Footlecrannoch, entering with a large tray. 'One lump or two?'

'Several,' said Horace. 'I'm dealing with amateurs here!'

Six

Vince and Horace sat drinking their very sweet tea and scratching their heads quite vigorously, like you do when you are thinking very, very hard.

Fenella and Carol were being no help whatsoever, and were licking the chocolate off the biscuits Mrs

Footlecrannoch had brought them at the same time as trying on all of her shoes.

'Thank goodness we chose this astute pair to come and help,' remarked Horace sarcastically. 'I can't think what we would do without their enquiring minds.'

'A working day with no beauty is an empty one,' said Fenella, sharply.

'What would you know about work?' growled Horace.

'Stop it, you two!' said Vince.

'I think I have a hunch . . .'

'Sounds painful,' said Carol, who was trying to squeeze one of her trotters into a rather fetching brogue.

Vince ignored her. 'I've been reviewing the evidence. Look at these two feathers – one black, one white. What bird springs to mind?'

'A black-and-white one,' answered Horace, knowingly.

'Indeed, my brilliant accomplice! And which birds can you think of that are black and white?'

'MAGPIES!' shrieked Fenella. 'Magpies! Oh, Vincey, you've solved it! You know, I've always suspected that it was a magpie who pinched my mother's tiara! They simply adore anything shiny by all accounts! You've hit the nail on the head, you deliciously clever if rather scruffy human!'

Just then Janet the owl and

Hamish the eagle flooped, flupped
and ferlipped their way on to the
windowsill, cawing and cooing
loudly. They had been given the
job of 'lookouts', but had suddenly
realised they had no idea what they

were meant to be looking out for.

'We've suddenly realised we have no idea what we are meant to be looking out for, el capitans!' squawked Janet, saluting.

'Och aye – nooo idea a' orl,' added Hamish.

'It's a magpie!' Vince exclaimed excitedly, pointing to the incriminating feathers. 'Look! Our theory so far is that a magpie has stolen Mrs F.'s jewels.'

'You brilliant boy!' exclaimed

Janet. 'Well, now that that's sorted, can we all go home? I haven't eaten for at least eight minutes, and this daylight is playing havoc with my peepers!' (Owls are night birds as a rule – I bet you knew that.)

'Aye, A'm exhausted tae,' said Hamish. 'A'm oot o' the habit o' soaring, an' Wesley ma keeper brangs ma lurnch soooon – besides, Fingers Malone is an unpleasant wee tyke, I dinnae wanna hav' tae deal wi' him!'

'Oh, the dedication you bring

to your work is humbling,' griped
Horace.

'Hang on!' said Vince. 'Fingers
Malone? Who's that?'

'He's the extremely dodgy magpie
who nests in that big plane tree
behind the zoo's customer
toilets,' said Janet.

'Oh my days!'
exclaimed Fenella.
'He's probably sitting
on Mother's tiara too –
what a turn-up!'

'I'm afraid we are going to have to send you on this part of the investigation, due to you both having wings,' said Vince to Janet and Hamish.

'She's got wings too!' said Janet, pointing one of hers at Fenella accusingly.

'Ah yes, but I don't do flying!' retorted Fenella. 'It

makes me perspire and that's not good for my complexion, don't you know!'

(Isn't she a hoot, dear reader? I'm still working on getting her snooty song in somewhere – fingers crossed the Powers That Be allow it!)

At this point Mrs Footlecrannoch came to collect the tea tray. Janet and Hamish hid behind the curtains.

'How is it progressing up here? Any leads?' she asked hopefully, failing to notice that Carol was now wearing TWO pairs of her shoes.

'As a matter of fact, yes!' said Vince proudly. 'We are about to follow up one now, Mrs F. We'll report back as soon as we can. Meanwhile, please do not touch the scene of the crime . . . in case we are barking up the wrong tree!' he added to amuse himself.

'Indeed, I wouldn't dream of it. Your team members don't have much to say for themselves,' she remarked suspiciously.

'They're from . . . Land's End!' said Vince. It was the furthest-away place he had ever been to. 'They don't understand the lingo,' he added nervously.

'That explains it!' said Mrs Footlecrannoch sagely, as she swept out of the room feeling utterly baffled. 'Do let yourselves out!'

Seven

At that moment, dear reader, Fingers Malone the magpie was pottering about his nest, having a bit of a dust and a dance, quietly singing the latest pop song he had heard. He was very partial to a bit of popular music.

FLOOOOOOSH! SWOOOOSH! FLIMPER FLIMPER PHOOOOF!

Suddenly, Hamish and Janet
landed on the branch beside him in
a firework of feathers.

'Jeepers!' exclaimed Fingers, nearly falling off his nest with surprise. 'To what do I owe the pleasure of this ominous visitation?!' he added anxiously. (Hamish was looking particularly large and bald-eagley.)

'We've come with a warrant to search your nest!' said Janet sternly, though she hoped that Fingers wouldn't ask to see the warrant, as she was fibbing about that bit.

'Whatever for?' said Fingers, somewhat nervously.

'Ahhh, that would be telling!' Janet hooted mysteriously. Then she added all in one breath:

'If you must know: there's been a jewel robbery and there was a black feather and a white feather at the

scene of the crime so we deduced
with our razor-sharp minds that
YOU are the culprit PLUS you're
the only thief we know so hand it
all over now and we'll say no more
about it make it snappy this crime-
solving's exhausting you have
the right to call your lawyer but I
wouldn't recommend it as I've heard
it costs an arm and a leg and you
don't even HAVE arms or legs.'

'Well, that's rich!' said Fingers,
looking rather dejected. 'I gave up

the world of petty thievery years ago. Crime doesn't pay,' he added mournfully.

'A likely story, you tyke!' said Janet huffily.

'Aye, a likely story! Och aye the absoloot noo!' interjected Hamish, who felt he hadn't really contributed much so far.

AYE! I MEAN YES, A LIKELY STORY!

Vince shouted from the bottom of the tree, where the rest of the team were lurking, all rather wishing they had wings.

'LIKELY INDEED! WHERE'S MY MUM'S TIARA TOO, YOU UTTER SCOUNDREL?!' shrieked Fenella, going even pinker than usual with the effort.

'OINK!' oinked Carol, feeling she really ought to pig up, I mean pipe up.

'Once a tea leaf, always a tea leaf . . .' said Horace half-heartedly. He was starting to find the whole affair rather tedious.

Fingers Malone felt surrounded. It took him back to his days as a lowlife and it made him shudder. He took a deep breath and reminded himself how much he had changed and at what cost. 'Go on then, search my home. I have nothing to hide,' he said proudly.

Hamish and Janet searched . . . Fingers wasn't lying. His home was surprisingly minimalist for a magpie, and the only glittery thing they found was the green foil wrapper from a mint choc biscuit.

'I told you so,' Fingers Malone said virtuously.

'Anything coming to light up there, gumshoe chums?' Vince yelped, feeling distinctly cut off from the action. He had tried to climb the tree, but due to its lack of lower branches had had to throw in the trowel – I mean towel.

'Nothing to declare, el capitans!' squawked Janet.

'Aye, thir's noo evidence tae be

 seen!' exclaimed Hamish, wondering if he could take an extended lunch break now.

'I don't think I can cope with all this excitement,' grumbled Horace, eyeing up a juicy grub he'd just spotted.

The walkie-talkie crackled into life.

'One two, one two – Asquith and the home team here. Is it all going spiffingly well, comrades? Is it all done and dusted? Have you put the tin lid on the whole ghastly affair? Has good triumphed over evil? Can we all once again sleep soundly in our igloos?'

'Don't be absurd!' Vince exclaimed crossly as he snatched the walkie-talkie from Fenella. 'This is a complicated business. We are in the process of following up some other leads.'

'Are we?!' the team chorused

'Yes, we are! Back to Mrs

Footlecrannoch's and step on it, there's no time to lose! The plot has thickened!'

'I beg to differ,' muttered Horace.

'Hey! Don't I deserve an apology?' Fingers Malone shouted after them, feeling somewhat hard done by.

Nobody heard him. He sat in his nest and quietly sang a sad little song.

'Even though the night is dark,

And day is very light,

It's hard to say that anything

Is really black or white.

I know I am,

It's clear to see,

But that's just feathers

Covering me.

Inside I'm other colours too . . .

The one I'm feeling now is blue.'

Eight

Our intrepid team of super sleuths were soon back at Mrs Footlecrannoch's. She let them in rather distractedly, as she had just settled down to watch her daily diet of quiz shows on the telly and was in the middle of trying to work out a particularly thorny anagram.

'Right – let's focus,' said Vince, suddenly taking himself very seriously.

'You're taking yourself very seriously,' observed Horace.

'Somebody has to!' Vince barked unexpectedly. He was feeling hungry now, which always made him a bit grumpy. He couldn't stop thinking about the lashings of Swiss roll that at this moment seemed gravely out of reach. 'Focus, team – focus on the clues we have left . . .'

Horace closed his eyes to try to look focused, but really he was grabbing forty winks.

Fenella and Carol dispensed with any remnants of the control they had exercised earlier and began sucking the fillings out of all Mrs Footlecrannoch's chocolates, giggling uncontrollably.

Hamish and Janet began comparing tail feathers on the windowsill.

Vince stared at a sticky trail on the floor, thinking – properly 'deducing', actually—

'SLUG!'

Horace awoke with a start. 'PARDON!?!' he spluttered.

'Don't be rude!' said Fenella.

Carol choked on a strawberry cream.

Hamish and Janet looked

interested at last – they were quite partial to a juicy slug.

'It's a slug trail! That stickiness there on the carpet, leading from the jewellery box . . . It's a slug trail!' said Vince excitedly, with Swiss rolls reflected in his eyes. 'We just need to follow the slug trail – it could lead to some answers.'

'I think it's safe to say it could lead to a slug,' said Horace knowingly.

The trail led across Mrs Footlecrannoch's swirly carpet and up and out of the window – but since none of them could walk down walls, our cunning team let themselves out of Mrs F.'s back door and into her wilderness of a garden. They picked up the trail by the downpipe of Mrs F.'s dodgy-looking guttering.

Fenella and Carol were beginning to feel very drowsy, thanks to their coming down from the sugar rush caused by snaffling too many chocs.

Janet and Hamish also fancied a snooze, and were now perched in a cherry tree, going to sleep. (To be fair to Janet, it was well past her usual bedtime.)

'The sharpness of our team is really quite overwhelming,' droned Horace.

Just then Vince (who frankly was the only one still in crime-solving mode) called everyone to order 'Right, team! Caution at all times. Lie low and follow me – I can literally smell the Swiss roll already!' He got down on to all fours, whipped out his magnifying glass (which he didn't really need, but it looked the part) and began following the sticky slug trail along Mrs Footlecrannoch's crazy paving.

Horace and Carol didn't need to get down on all fours as they were already down on them, as it were. Fenella couldn't, as she didn't really have arms, so she clip-clopped along at the back making snooty remarks about Mrs F.'s garden, 'I've always thought crazy paving was sooo last year' being one of them.

'I feel we are getting warmer, team,' Vince said encouragingly from inside a huge rhododendron bush.

'I certainly am,' said Horace. 'This

isn't a garden, this is the countryside
– my little legs are killing me.'

The walkie-talkie crackled
once more. 'Dudes!
What's occurring?
Just to say you are
in for a treat with
the entertainment
tonight! Not giving
anything away but
Vince's gran knows her onions when
it comes to natty moves, man! Over.'

'BINGO!!!' shrieked Vince.

'No man! Bingo ain't happening –
much cooler stuff than Bingo! Over.'

'No, I mean BINGO! Over and
out!!!'

For there before them, looking
very shamefaced, was a rather
rotund slug wearing a huge ruby
ring around his girth.

Nine

'Hello, I'm Wayne. Oooh, crikey – you've got me bang to rights! It's a fair cop, guvnor, I'll come quietly – please, no cuffs . . .'

Vince was having to try very hard to look serious and sleuthy, as in all honesty he was longing to guffaw. A slug wearing a ruby ring – let's face it, that is quite a funny thing. But Horace, Carol and Fenella went to no effort at all to keep up their sleuthy status, and were all hanging on to each other, weak with mirth.

Vince just about managed to keep control. 'Where's the rest of

the booty, you sneaky slug!?' he exclaimed.

'I can't possibly divulge that,' Wayne replied pathetically.

'You must and you will! My gran has been implicated in this dastardly crime, and we are here to clear her good name, you scoundrel!' (Vince felt that mentioning the Swiss roll here might sound a tad shallow, so he kept shtoom on that point.)

'I just wanted to be beautiful for a moment, to sparkle, and so I

got caught up in the dark side . . .
I mustn't squeal – they'll tear me
to shreds!'

'Who's "they"?' Vince quizzed
him.

'We need to go somewhere
private,' Wayne whispered. 'I promise
to spill the beans if you spare me.
I've never stolen nuffink before, I've
always lived a very moral life . . . for
a slug.'

'One two, one two, calling Super-
Sleuth Team!!' The walkie-talkie

suddenly pankled very loudly into action. 'Terry and the home team talking – what's going down, dudes? We miss you, man – any luck? We are so ready to entertain you, Daddy-Os! Over.'

'We are coming back with our first suspect for interrogation, Terry – get the interrogation room ready! Over,' Vince said with vigour into the walkie-talkie, giving a flamboyant flick of his red cape.

'Interrogation room, man?!

What's that when it's at home? Over.'

Vince blushed and shot a look at Wayne, who luckily didn't seem to be taking the conversation in, and was quietly oozing his sluggy body free of the ruby ring.

'You know . . . the interrogation room!' Vince hissed. 'Your enclosure will do – make it look sparse and intimidating. Over.'

'It already looks like that, man! Roger, wilko, see you all soon, bros! Over.'

Janet and Hamish, who had been asleep on the cherry tree all this time and managed to miss everything, were woken by Terry's tones whootling walkie-talkie style around the garden. They flooped over to the team and landed gracefully on Carol's back, spotting immediately with their eagle (and owl) eyes Wayne and the glistening ruby ring now at his side.

'Och aye the noo! Is tha' a rrrubee rang A spy thir by that slug?' said Hamish.

'I'm frightfully partial to a slug!' added Janet, dribbling a bit.

'This is our VALUABLE major suspect, WAYNE!' said Vince quickly – making sure he emphasised the words VALUABLE and WAYNE (not even owls eat slugs that have names). 'We are taking him back to the zoo for interrogation. He knows things.'

Carol and Fenella suddenly chimed in, having finally recovered from their giggles, and wanting some attention.

'WE know things!'

'Yes, but nothing of any use,' said Horace bluntly.

Vince picked Wayne up on a large leaf, carefully pocketed the ruby ring and led the unlikely team back to the zoo.

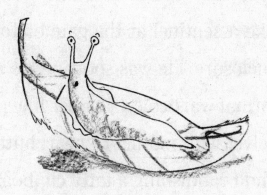

Ten

When they arrived back at the
zoo, they found Asquith standing
like a sentinel at the gate of Terry's
enclosure. He was sporting his most
formal waistcoat (a rather fine plum
velvet with mother-of-pearl buttons)
and brandishing a tatty clipboard.

'This way, please, you beastly

felon!' he snapped, adding, 'Hang on a bally mo . . . where is the felon?'

'What's a felon, dude?' asked Terry, who was attaching a small sign he had made out of scraps of newspaper to the bars of his cage:

'I'll tell you later,' Asquith whispered out of the corner of his beak.

Vince held Wayne aloft. 'Here he is!'

'Oh!' Terry snorted. 'That's a very tiny "felon", man. Yo!'

'Don't be decieved by his size,' Horace blustered.

'Yes! He's clearly a master criminal, and he undoubtedly belongs to a notorious underworld gang!' said Vince.

'Ahoy there, whipper- snappers! Innocent until proven guilty!' Gran chirruped as she approached with some homemade apple juice. 'I thought you super sleuths might have worked up a thirst.'

While Carol and Fenella and Hamish and Janet made a bee- line for the beverages, Terry and Asquith led Vince and Wayne into the intimidating enclosure/ interrogation room.

Juan the llama and Dave the goat were already in there, with their hooves formally crossed and plastic police helmets on their heads.

Wayne told his story under the beady gaze of the gang.

He had been seduced into the thieving deed by two beautiful Siamese cats called Selina and Lavinia, who lived next door to Mrs Footlecrannoch. He had overheard them talking about how they could get away with anything because they were so beautiful – no one ever suspected them of being wicked, so they could use this to their advantage to steal Mrs Footlecrannoch's jewels

and become even more beautiful. Beauty was power and jewels were wealth – and they would rule the Siamese cat world with iron claws.

Wayne had had no such grand desires. He just longed for even a tiny morsel of their allure.

'Gotta say I've never been partial to cats,' Dave muttered to Juan, who was busy picking his dodgy gnashers with a picnic fork he had found on the floor. 'All that purring. I find it so pretentious.'

Fenella, who had now supped her own body weight in juice and clip-clopped in to hear the lowdown, piped up. 'Beauty and power, beauty and power – yes, well, I've got BOTH in spades, darlings, what can I tell you? It's almost a curse.'

'Oh do shut up, you big-head!' Horace hissed under his breath.

'So these nasty thieving felines clearly need catching!' said Vince, rather pleased with his simple deduction.

'Oooh, feeeeline felons!' said Juan, clicking his heels with satisfaction.

Asquith, who had been very quiet up till now, scribbling frantically on his clipboard, suddenly spoke up.

'I happen to know cats LOVE fish and HATE water . . . and I have plenty of both! Gather round! I appear to have hatched a brilliant plan, my furry, feathery friends!'

Eleven

Hamish and Janet were perched in Mrs Footlecrannoch's cherry tree with a bucket of water from Asquith's pond precariously balanced beside them.

(Have you ever carried water in a bucket? I suspect you have – it is a surprisingly heavy affair, isn't it?)

Terry, who had been cunningly disguised as a bush by Gran, sat stock-still immediately beneath them with a pile of smelly mackerel at his feet – courtesy again of Asquith and his stash of tea time treats.

Carol and Fenella, who had insisted on coming even though they were offering

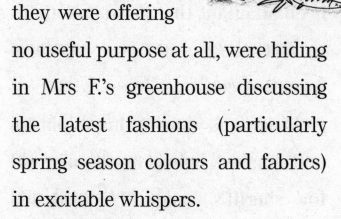

no useful purpose at all, were hiding in Mrs F.'s greenhouse discussing the latest fashions (particularly spring season colours and fabrics) in excitable whispers.

Juan and Dave were posted in the passage at the side of the house, just in case the pesky cats slipped from Terry's mighty grasp. They were quietly practising the nifty dance moves they had learnt from Gran that morning. (Dave had also been adamant that he wasn't about to miss the capture of a couple of conceited cats.)

Vince was wearing Juan's plastic policeman's helmet and an old toy sheriff's badge. He and his trusty sidekick Horace (both still in their red and black capes) had secreted themselves somewhat unsuccessfully behind a rather nasty garden statue of a small boy having a wee (dear reader, I think this statue was meant to be some sort of fountain, but it had long since ceased to work/wee).

Suspected felon Wayne was back at the zoo under the watchful eye of Asquith, and Gran (who had refused to go anywhere near

Mrs Footlecrannoch's) had gone to change into party clothes and prep some top snacks, as she was convinced there would soon be something to celebrate.

The plan was plotted, hatched and poised.

Asquith's Very Brilliant Penguiny
Plan

Disguise Terry as a bush —
thank you, Gran, costume lady!

Lure Selina and Lavinia the
baddy cats with stinky makerel.
(Bleugh!)

Douse them in Asquith's pond
water from above (to be done by
Janet and Hamish in tree with
bucket of aforementioned liquid).

Terry/bush to grab disorientated
soggy catty baddies.

Citizens arrest by yours truly and my trusty side order, I mean sidekick the heroic Horace.

Fenella and Carol standing by to look lovely.

Juan and Dave to provide moral support and to block escape route with their eight legs — and to lend me a policeman's helmet obvs.

Sorted!

With the heady scent of not-very-fresh mackerel playing upon their respective noses, they all kept as quiet as they could . . .

and waited . . .

and waited . . .

and waited . . .

After about an hour and thirty-eight and a half minutes, once Juan had practised his dance steps so much his hooves hurt;

and Dave had retold all of his dodgy goat jokes;

and Carol and Fenella had exhausted their favourite topic, and begun to bicker a bit about who were the best designers and why;

and Hamish and Janet were both suffering from extreme cramp;

and Terry badly needed the loo;

and Horace and Vince were starting to drop

off, having been playing endless
I spy—

There was a rittle-rittle-rootle and
a frithy-frith-fatootle in the hedge.

'Selina, it's definitely getting
closer, dear – purrrrr! Mackerel,
if I'm not mistaken . . .'

'Oh, Lavinia – that is my utter
favourite, purrrrr! Manna from
heaven! What luck! I do hope it's
filleted!'

And there they were, sparkling
in the twilight – two beautiful, sleek

Siamese cats, one wearing pearls and one wearing diamonds, self-satisfied heads held high, and snaky tails waving like furry unfurled flags behind them.

Our hiding team were suddenly on utter tenterhooks . . .

Breaths were tightly bated . . .

Closer and closer to Terry's fishy toes they got . . .

The tension was palpable . . .

The atmosphere was taut with anticipation . . .

You could have heard a pip squeak . . .

And then – horribly, suddenly, and with the speed of a frantic bullet – Terry let out the most EXPLOSIVE FART you have

ever

ever

ever

ever

ever

ever heard!

Hamish and Janet shrieked like banshees and let go of the bucket, which landed with a splash and a clatter on Terry's leafy head.

Fenella and Carol legged it out of the greenhouse just in time to be showered with Asquith's pongy pond water, and to completely get in the

way of Vince and Horace, who, with their capes flapping furiously, ended up barking out the words they had rehearsed as a dynamic duo – 'Stop, wretched thieves! We arrest you in the name of decency and fair play!' – into Carol and Fenella's generous bottoms.

Meanwhile, amidst the hullabaloo, Juan and Dave galloped heroically, like veritable stallions, towards Selina and Lavinia (who had been so gassed by Terry's fart they had both partially fainted) and managed to grab one each with their generous gnashers – unexpectedly saving the day!

So you see, dear reader, sometimes things can work out really well . . . even if they don't go quite according to plan!

Twelve

Lavinia and Selina were holding on to the bars of Janet's leafy enclosure, looking damp and pathetic, and

still feeling a bit woozy from Terry's intense bottom gases.

Gerry the local copper had been duly called, and was standing next to Vince and Gran, struggling with the concept of questioning two cats as well as taking down a few particulars.

'I must apologise, Mrs Ligglethwaite – I think I might have appeared rather rude earlier when I was eyeing up your copious collection of rocks,' he muttered, slightly grudgingly.

'No matter, young man!' replied Gran, fluttering her eyelashes. 'Do call me Genevieve!' she added, thinking quietly that 'Gerry and Genevieve' had quite a nice ring to it . . .

'So a citizen's arrest, you say . . . I see,' said Gerry (fortified by Gran's charm). 'Lured by mackerel, caught red-pawed, still sporting snaffled booty. Unusual. Cat burglars, quite literally! Ha ha ha!'

'Yes! Ha ha!' Vince chimed in, rather annoyed that he hadn't spotted the obvious gag.

'A very obvious gag . . . how gauche,' remarked Horace under his breath.

'There is a reward, you know,

Vince,' Gerry said, smiling. 'Swiss roll – apparently all you can eat!' he added with a grin.

'So I heard,' said Vince nonchalantly, trying to sound uninterested, whilst his treacherous stomach rumbled the national anthem. 'Oh! And we found this, too!' he chirruped, as he suddenly remembered the ruby ring. He fished it out from deep within his pocket to show Gerry.

'Wow! That's some rock, isn't it, Vince?!' said Gerry. 'Did our captured cat burglars make away with that as well?' (Gerry smugly chuckled once again at his feline quip, which was really very galling.)

'No, actually my very good-looking mate Wayne found it . . . erm, just knocking about in the grass! They must have dropped it, I suppose . . .'

'Well done, Good-Looking Wayne! Quite a day! Right, I'll get these cat burglars in the van, ha ha ha!' (Vince thought he was really pushing it now.) 'I suspect you would like to go and claim your well-deserved reward, young man. We could do with a detective of your calibre down at the station,' Gerry added kindly with a wink.

Meanwhile Wayne was blushing quite pink. (I don't think I've ever seen a blushing slug, dear reader – have you?) No one had ever referred to him as 'good-looking' before.

It had been agreed that Vince and Horace should fetch the Swiss roll and return the jewels, whilst everyone else (under Asquith and Terry's supervision) prepared for the celebration party.

Dingley dongley dannger lannger bongey bungey raddley ruddley beeeeeep! went Mrs Footlecrannoch's ridiculously flamboyant bell.

She appeared in her fishy specs and wearing a very jaunty trilby hat, but looking a tad forlorn. Then she spotted what Vince and Horace were carrying.

'Bless my giddy soul!' Mrs Footlecrannoch exclaimed, and her big eyes lit up as salty tears began to run down her craggy cheeks. 'You've found it all! My pride and joys, gifted to me by my seventh husband, Anton Brimbramble St John the second, Mayor of Clacton-on-Sea! He was an utter cad, but how I LOVED him!'

Then she took the ring and necklaces from Vince's hands and immediately put them all on.

'Swiss roll all round!' she shrieked. 'I made it myself from an ancient recipe of my fifth mother-in-law's. She was a wonderfully experimental cook from Grimsby.' She swooped down her long hallway to fetch it.

'Can you be experimental with Swiss roll?' whispered Horace, rather hoping that you couldn't.

Mrs Footlecrannoch returned swiftly, carrying an enormous plate decorated with brown flowers and with a huge, worryingly green and grey, sausagey-looking sponge placed upon it.

'Congratulations, jubilations, celebrations unconfined! Enjoy! I shall be ever gratefully yours! Please don't bother returning the plate. I have always found it repellent!'

And with that Mrs Footlecrannoch shut the door rather abruptly in their faces.

'Well! That was rather abrupt – and I don't know about you, but if that's

a Swiss roll then I'm the manager
of Tottenham Hotspur,' chuntered
Horace.

Number of criminals caught: 2!

Number of jewels returned: 3!

Number of yummy-looking Swiss rolls
lavished on the super sleuths as
a reward: 0!

Thirteen

Vince and Horace returned to the zoo in the twilight, carrying the revolting-looking experimental Swiss roll aloft. There they found everyone sitting around Wayne (who in turn was sitting on Carol as if she was a piggy stage), listening to his story.

'Yes, I'm just a humble gastropod.

But we are the second largest species in the animal kingdom, in terms of our marvellous diversity,' he declared, endeavouring to look extra shiny.

'Oooh, what's the first, pray tell?' asked Fenella in her poshest voice. 'I've a fabulous hunch it's flamingos – in so many ways we are first class!'

she added pompously.

'It's insects!' replied Wayne.

'INSECTS!?' everyone chorused with genuine surprise.

'Yes! And I'm a vital part of the ecosystem!' continued Wayne proudly. 'But I'm not very popular, and humans are always trying to kill me.'

'Welcome to my world!' said Carol, 'Ever heard of bacon? The zoo saved mine!'

'Move in with us, why don't you,

you charming fellow? – I mean slug,' remarked Asquith, suddenly feeling very full-hearted and public-spirited.

'Yay, dude, move in, man – this is deffo the place to hang!' Terry said.

'Aye, mak' yersel' a' home, wee McWayne!' Hamish said.

'It would be madness not to, you lowly chap,' said Fenella, rather rudely.

'T'whit, t'whoo!' hooted Janet, who was still rather depressed that she would have to forgo eating him.

'Got any good slug jokes?' Dave asked.

'You've certainly moved on to me already!' said Carol with a heady mix of pleasure and slight irritation.

'Eet seems your fate eeeees seeeealed, darlink sluggy theeeeng,' said Juan (rather ominously!).

Vince, who up to this point hadn't wanted to butt in, gave a polite cough. Everyone swung round to be confronted with Vince and Horace and the utterly revolting-looking cake.

'Check this out – Swiss roll, my aunt Fanny!' Horace barked. 'For this I have spent the day fraternising with the underworld of petty thievery,' he added bitterly.

'BLEEEAUGH!' they all chorused

with feeling.

'When I said I could eat a blinkin'
horse, I certainly didn't mean one
that looked as green and mouldy as
THAT!' spluttered Dave!

'I think I might beeee seeeek!'
moaned Juan, which reminded
everyone of his ditty from earlier
in the day.

Suddenly, they all heard an
approaching 'Yoooooo hoooooo!'

It was Gran, who, knowing full
well that Mrs Footlecrannoch would

likely disappoint (well, actually –
more to the point – had been rather
HOPING she would), had been
baking like a loony most of the day.
Now she was pushing a hostess
trolley heaped with a giddy array of
delicious-looking cakes and pastries,
and Vince's dad was following
behind with the pièce de résistance
– the biggest Swiss roll any of them
had ever seen!

Gran's grin was ridiculously
wide, she was sporting a huge lacy

apron over a violet-and-lime Lycra
one-piece and – you've guessed it! –
more jewellery than you could shake
a stick at.

Vince gasped and suddenly ran
off very swiftly towards the toilets.

'Nature calls, clearly . . . muttered Horace.

But in no time Vince was back, and who should be sitting on his shoulder but . . . Fingers Malone, looking rather rosy for a black-and-white bird.

'On behalf of everyone here, Fingers, I should like to publicly apologise for our clumsy and unfriendly accusations. Please do us the honour of joining us for our celebration?'

'Apology accepted. Yes please!' Fingers said with a grateful grin.

'Now we can party!' exclaimed Vince with delight.

Fourteen

Terry appeared rather theatrically from Asquith's igloo and made an announcement via his walkie-talkie. 'Take a seat, my dudey friends – let the entertainments commence!'

Every sleuth chose a cake from Gran's trolley, and then they were ushered to their seats (or logs) by

Asquith, who was still sporting his velvet waistcoat, and had since added a blue polka-dot cravat.

Then Asquith tapped his ice-cream-stick baton on the wall;

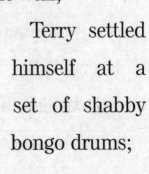

Terry settled himself at a set of shabby bongo drums;

And Juan, Dave and Gran emerged from the igloo, all beaming from ear to ear and clearing their throats. (Well, it is a story with songs, remember . . . and dances, come to think of it.)

♪ THE SUPER—SLEUTH SONG
(and dance)

♩♫

You are the bestest super sleuths!

Of you we are soooooo proud!

♩

You've got the looks,

you've got the youth,

Forensically you've found the truth.

Returned the jewels to that silly old cow,

Gran wrote that line, dear reader!

Gosh golly whoopee doo and wow!!!

♩

You are the brains, you are the brawn,

𝅘𝅥 Of you we are amazed!

You followed the leads,

you unwrapped the clues,

Gran wanted
to call her
something Now Mrs F.'s not got the blues.
rude here too
but no one
would let her.
They said once
was enough!

158

The jewels are returned to

their rightful place,

Bet you can't wipe that smug grin

from your face!

You are soo clever, soo witty and brave,

Of you we are in awe!

You rose to the challenge,

the nettle you grasped,

Our expectations are well surpassed.

The task is a triumph,

we think you'll agree,

Yippety yippety, bundles of glee!

We are soo happy, we are soo glad,

We make a mighty team.

You out solving crimes

and being soo canny,

Us here writing rhymes

and dancing with Granny!

It's a triumph all round,

what a red-letter day!!

Three cheers for us all —

hip hip hip HOOORAY!!!

And with that Juan, Dave and Gran took eight very deep bows, as the audience erupted into reckless applause. Gran collapsed, chortling and exhausted.

'More cake, anyone?' she tootled weakly.

There was a collective squeal of 'YES!'

'I quite fancy the look of that green one,' said Wayne, eyeing up the dodgy Swiss roll. 'It smells of rotting veg – my favourite!'

There was another collective squeal of 'IT'S ALL YOURS!'

'Told you I was good for the ecosystem!' said Wayne, and he happily tucked in.

Epilogue

So, dear reader, we have reached the end of this adventure.

A long and eventful day in the lives of both our human and our animal friends.

Mrs Footlecrannoch falls asleep wearing her rescued jewellery, with a smile playing across her skew-

whiff lips.

Gerry the local copper lies awake with a wry grin on his face as he replays his cat-burglar gag over and over in his head.

And what of the cat burglars themselves, Lavinia and Selina, the cats who turned to crime? After a very stern warning Gerry let them off – perhaps foolishly, dear reader, for right at this moment they are preening themselves on a warm brick wall in the moonlight, discussing what they might get away with next… Some people/cats never learn.

The rest of our animals snuffle and sniffle and scuffle and drobble down into their enclosures, as if they were ordinary zoo animals who hadn't just had such an extraordinary day.

Our new friend Wayne proudly hunkers down amidst Carol the pig's fantastically messy pen and congratulates himself on rejecting a life of thieving and skullduggery.

Dad, Gran and Vince sing their way along the winding zoo paths to their back gate, and Dad tells Vince how proud he is of his super sleuthing and how very well he can carry off a pillar-box red cape.

And as they pass his nest, Fingers Malone sings a little lullaby to himself . . .

'Even though the night is dark

my heart feels full of light!

Sometimes a day can start all wrong

and turn out very right.

I stood accused,

but they were wrong,

so now my spirit

turns to song!

The colour blue changed in a wink . . .

The one I'm feeling now is . . . pink!'

If there was a moral to this story, dear reader – which there isn't, but if there was – it would be that looks are overrated . . . and character is all.

Oh, and just before he fell asleep, Vince wrote a Wayne-sized entry in Derek . . .

Mission accomplished!!

THE END

Oh, dear reader! One more thing
– I nearly forgot!

The Powers That Be said we
could have a reprise in the form of
Fenella's song. I do hope you like it.

FENELLA'S SONG

Ooh do look up at me,

I'm a speciality!

Wouldn't you say so?

The body of a stork

And a goose's feet, but then

We surprise the world times ten,

With our pink plummage!

Hooga hooga yar!

Hooga hooga yar!

Check out that plummage!

Oooh the silly fools

they think

That our ankles be

our knees –

How very wrong.

Tee hee tee hee!

It makes us chortle.

To think our ankle is our knee –

How very stupid can they be?

Stinka stinka parf!

Stinka stinka parf!

They are sooo stupid!

Ooh we love so much to wade,

And we don't even get paid.

It's just our pleasure,

To cross the muddy flats.

We love to suck the silt

And sieve crustaceans with our bills,

Like finding treasure.

Brinka brinka honk!

Brinka brinka honk!

Such precious treasure!

Flamboyance is our game,

(If we're in a flock the name,)

Oh, don't you know it.

Our brains are smaller than our eyes

But don't be misled

By the size –

We are quite BRILLIANT.

Ginja ginja flamp!

Ginga ginga flamp!

Modest but BRILLIIIIIIANT!

Acknowledgements

For the ladies and gents at Faber

my thanks it has no bounds.

If it weren't for them Vince and his

friends

would never have been found . . .

Leah and Alice and Nimmy,

Hannah and Susan and Em,

all of the nifty sales team,

everyone a gem!

Rebecca A I remember the day

I saw her drawn eyes shine.

That she wanted to play

made me shout hip hooray,

more than once more than twice, many

times . . .

A special thanks must be

For fabby Tate Petrie

Whose extra pics are soo

fantabulous and spesh

I know she's mad for art

For bats & hats, strawb tart

She's also partial to canoes

And climbing in delicious shoes

I wave the flag of glee T.P

That you should gift such craft to me.

Curtis Brown you are up town

and clever as can be.

Thank you Lauren, Steph, Becca & Em

for sooooo looking after me . . .

Dear readers, most of all,

I must thank you tenfold.

I hope you're glad you bought this book,

I hope you liked the tale it told,

of Vince, of Dad, of Gran, of all

the characters within the zoo.

From Sophie T and all of them,

we doff our caps to all of you!

Have you read Vince's
first adventure?

ZOO BOY

SOPHIE
THOMPSON

ILLUSTRATED BY REBECCA ASHDOWN